Drawings by the Fernbank Elementary School students featured in this book
Majii and the Mountain Gorillas of Rwanda

Jed Augustine	Sarah Barger	Anne Boring
Amelia Blumberg	Brittany Bromfield	Raianna Brown
Parker Ciliax	Cara Lynn Clarkson	Sarah Dasher
Paige Epps	Shayla Fant	Demario Flowers
William Gardner	Indigo Gordon	Pera Hardy
Alex Hasken	Nate Henneman	Sarah Hudson
Rosie Hughes	Yardley Ingram	Zoe Jordan
Sydney Ann Lewis	Ruthie Lichtenstein	Ryan Linehan
Matthew Martin	Gabriel Nahmias	Maggie Nolen
Brianna Poovey	Matthew Richelo	Ethan Sawyer
Haoying Shi	Will Smith	Clay Tinkler
Claire Vastola	Shelby Wardlaw	Austin Weatherly
	Hannah Wichmann	

Drawings on the Mountain Gorillas of Rwanda by the Fernbank Elementary School students displayed at
Hartsfield Youth Art Gallery, Concourse E, International Terminal
Hartsfield International Airport, Atlanta
March – May, 2000

Sheereen Brown	Isaac Cady	Ben Evans
Celia Favorite	Dana Florkowski	Malaïka Gutekunst
Kelsey Knight	Aiva Leff	Jane Neiswander
Diana Peterman	Kate Phelps	Jah Ramsey
Tyler Slack	Stuart Spangler	John Speno
Abraham Taylor	Laura Toulme	Casondra Turner
Gabbie Watts		Alexandria White

Drawings on the Mountain Gorillas of Rwanda by the Fernbank Elementary School students displayed at
State Capitol Art Exhibit, Atlanta
January 29 – February 26, 2000

Kerry Ayres Smith
Nicole DeFrancis

PREFACES

Atlanta January 17, 2000

The mountain gorillas of Rwanda live in a beautiful mountain forest. When they visit the edges of their habitat in the Volcanoes National Park, they can see and hear the people who live in local villages as they work in their fields around the boundaries of the park.

The people are recovering and rebuilding in the aftermath of a devastating war and genocide. The children of Rwanda will be very pleased to know that children in Atlanta care about them, as well as the mountain gorillas who share their land.

Mountain gorillas are very like humans. They live in family groups and the adults are loving and protective parents. The infant gorillas and juveniles, called "blackbacks," love to play and climb trees and chase each other. They also like to wrestle with the adults in the group and can often be seen climbing all over the enormous silverback leader of the group. Just like humans, they only get away with this for a short period of time and then the silverback removes them so firmly that they are not tempted to return. At least not for a while! The mountain gorilla's natural disposition is calm and non-threatening, but again, like humans, they will fiercely protect their family and their territory from intruders.

To see a mountain gorilla in the wild is an unforgettable experience. You leave determined to protect their habitat and to help them survive.
However, not many people are lucky enough to see the mountain gorillas. Telling their story through Majii's adventures will help children all over the world to know them and to appreciate their right to share this planet with us. Then the children of the world can share this message with their parents so that many more families, communities, and schools will feel closer to the people and the gorillas of Africa.

I'm sure that the children and parents of Fernbank Elementary School already feel closer to the mountain gorillas.

Thank you so much for buying this book. You too are now part of the family!

Sincerely,

Clare Richardson
President & CEO
The Dian Fossey
Gorilla Fund International
Atlanta, Georgia, USA

The **Dian Fossey**
Gorilla Fund
International
Founded in Memory of Digit

FROM THE DESK OF AMBASSADOR JOSEPH MUTABOBA

New York, January 3, 2000

As a Rwanda Ambassador, I will start this preface by briefly introducing a dear friend and fellow Rwandan at heart. The author, Marc Daniel Gutekunst, was born in Butare (Rwanda) soon after his French parents arrived in Africa, where they dedicated 23 years of their career to education and health. They worked in Rwanda, Congo, and Burundi. His father, Dr. Daniel Gutekunst, is one of the founding members of the Université Adventsite de l'Afrique Centrale (Adventist University of Central Africa) in Rwanda, and founded the Kivoga Teachers Training College in Burundi. In 1968, at age ten, Marc Daniel visited with his childhood friends the Volcanoes National Park; they ran into elephants but never saw gorillas. Marc Daniel returned to Rwanda between 1979 and 1981 to conduct, under the supervision of the late Professor Albert Maurice, his fieldwork towards his bachelor's degree in zoology. He then worked in the Volcanoes National Park in Rwanda and the Kahuzi Biega National Park, in then Zaire. In 1981, he also directed an award-winning documentary film (December 1981) on Rwanda and the mountain gorillas entitled: *Au Rwanda, le Dernier Sanctuaire des Gorilles (In Rwanda: the Last Sanctuary of Gorillas)*. Eleven years later, he returned to work on HIV/AIDS with the Ministry of Health. In 1993, at the request of the Ministry of Health, he came back again to develop and establish a *Post War Development & Rehabilitation Program* implemented by ADRA Rwanda. On April 11, 1994, he left Kigali with the five just orphaned children of Prime Minister Agathe Uwilingiyimana, bringing them safely out of Africa. It is sad to note that the late Prime Minister and her husband, along with their blue beret Belgian bodyguards, were among the first victims of the genocide on April 7, 1994. A few months later, Marc Daniel returned to Rwanda to work with refugees and displaced populations.

I have had the privilege of knowing Stan Mullins for 6 years. Stan is an artist with humanism and a mission. He was the first renowned American painter to come to Rwanda. In 1993, he captured on his canvas the beauty of its countryside and the people, and returned in February-March 1994 to paint more and to display his work in Kigali, the capital city of Rwanda. The proceeds from the sales of this artwork went to the *Post War Development & Rehabilitation Program*. I commend him for the great work he did with the students from the Fernbank Elementary School. From the collage of the winning 37 drawings in this book, he skillfully conveyed his love for Rwanda and its endangered mountain gorillas to the children of Fernbank. Now we should have 654 young Rwandan Ambassadors in the State of Georgia and many more throughout America. I offer my thanks to all of you who will buy this book for your children and their friends all over the world.

When I left the Voice of America studios on May 19th, 1995, where I had been discussing the role of media during the 1994 Rwandan genocide, Marc Daniel and Stan shared with me their vision of MAJII during the opening of an art display in Atlanta of Stan's paintings on Rwanda. I was glad that they would both combine their talents and wealth of experiences and share them with children. Children are never too young to learn important life principles, such as protection of wildlife and reverence for life. Today's children will soon be forging new tomorrows for mankind and will continue to protect endangered species such as the mountain gorillas. In this past century, the world witnessed the worst wars and genocides, including the one in Rwanda of 1994, but the children at the beginning of this third millennium may be our best hope for peace and lasting prosperity.

In closing, I encourage all the readers of this book to pledge their contribution to making our global village-planet a better world where children and adults can live in peace and contribute to the conservation of unique ecosystems and wildlife.

Ambassador Joseph Mutaboba
Permanent Representative of Rwanda
To the United Nations, New York, USA
New York, New York, USA

Published by
FNT International Press
1534 North Decatur Road, Suite 204
Atlanta, Georgia 30307
USA

Printed in the United States of America
1st printing, February 2000

Library of Congress Catalog Card Number: 00-131214
ISBN 0-9679305-1-0 : $ 14.95

Gutekunst, Marc Daniel
Majii and the Mountain Gorillas of Rwanda / Marc Daniel Gutekunst
Illustrations by Stan Mullins & the Students of the Fernbank Elementary School, Atlanta, DeKalb County, Georgia

Summary: Majii, a drop of water, travels to the mountain tops of the Volcanoes National Park in Rwanda to meet the world's last mountain gorillas who share their plight for survival. Majii will also discover the impact the 1994 genocide had on the people of Rwanda and its wildlife. Majii leaves her newly found friends with a mission to encourage children around the world to start forging new tomorrows by protecting our fragile ecosystems and by nurturing their reverence of nature.

[1. Mountain gorillas—Fiction . 2. Rwanda—Fiction . 4. Conservation—Fiction . 5. Wildlife—Fiction . 6. War—Fiction .] I. Gutekunst, Marc Daniel, text. II. Mullins, Stan, ill. III. Students, Fernbank Elementary School, ill.

Book design by Lisa Durfee @ Durfee Design Group, Atlanta, Georgia, USA
Printing done by Apex Commercial Printing, Inc., Atlanta, Georgia, USA

MAJII AND THE MOUNTAIN GORILLAS OF RWANDA

by Marc Daniel Gutekunst

Illustrated by Stan Mullins
& The students of Fernbank Elementary School
Atlanta, DeKalb County, Georgia

FNT International Press
Atlanta, USA

"But why are you going, Majii?" asked Timba.

"I feel like discovering," answered Majii thoughtfully.

"Discovering what?"

"People! Animals! Forests! Cities!" exclaimed Majii breathlessly.

"You are nothing but one tiny drop of water!" reasoned Timba.

"How can you say that?" Majii said. "I can do anything! I've made up my mind to go."

"Just remember that we warned you about the dangers of traveling," Majii's friends said in chorus.

"Good-bye!" cried Majii.

What a tumble! Majii, a glistening drop of water, fell from a huge cloud. What a jump above a mountainous area surrounded by volcanoes, lakes, forests, and many small huts. Majii was falling into the heart of Africa, in fact, directly over the Volcanoes National Park of Rwanda. The air was chilly, and Majii could see for miles. A sudden wind carried the little water drop toward a grassy spot on the edge of a volcano. As she fell, Majii spotted a group of black hairy animals. The largest animal caught her attention.

"I think I'll land right on his face," Majii thought mischievously. Suddenly, Majii was on the animal's hairy cheeks. "What big eyes he has!" Majii thought.

"*Jambo*, Little One," said the animal.

"Hello," greeted the adventurous water drop. "My name is Majii, and I come from the country of Cloud Alto Cumulus Nimbus."

"I am Mukuru, the chief gorilla of this family," the big animal replied politely. "You just landed in the world's last gorilla home. Our home is a park."

"May I stay with you and visit your home?" Majii asked hopefully.

"Oh, that's not a problem, Majii," Mukuru replied.

"Thank you! Thank you!" Majii said, bouncing up and down on Mukuru's fuzzy face. Mukuru sat on the ground and sighed. He seemed sad. Holding out his big black palm he let Majii roll off his cheek like a tear.

"Sit here, Little One," said Mukuru in a deep voice. "Before I tell you everything about our families and our park, you should rest after your long trip. We will talk tomorrow."

"Yes, Mukuru, I must be well rested before I learn about your home and family," yawned Majii. Mukuru and his family chuckled. Mukuru made a bed for Majii out of a thick green leaf and some soft moss, and her little eyes closed. It had been a long day for Majii.

"Good night, Little One," Mukuru said softly.

Jambo means hello in Swahili, an African language

As the sun slowly rose in the distance, and the clouds moved away, the peak of the highest volcano, the Karisimbi, could be seen, snow-capped like a sugar-coated candy. Chirping birds flew through the clear air to land on the backs of mountain buffaloes grazing on the fringes of the clearing. A family of antelopes stopped to watch Mukuru's sleeping family and then trotted away. As the morning dew dried, the air warmed. One by one the gorilla family woke up. Some yawned and stretched their arms and legs while others walked around. Mukuru grunted. Then, all 12 family members gathered around him.

"We have a new friend who has traveled a long way to visit us. Please welcome Majii!" said Mukuru in his booming voice. "Let us introduce ourselves to Majii."

"May I start, Father?" said the youngest family member.

"Yes, of course," Mukuru answered.

"My name is Matata. I am always getting into trouble. One day soon I will be a silver back gorilla," said Matata with great pride.

"What is a silver back?" asked Majii.

"Silver backs are usually family leaders. Look at my back," answered Mukuru.

"Wow, çan you tell me more about your families?" asked Majii.

"Usually a gorilla family can have from three to 36 members, usually a father and mother and several generations of children," said Mukuru. "Its size depends on the abundance of food and the leader's character. Some leaders prefer small families." He paused, then added sadly: "It is easy to keep an eye on everyone in my family now, especially since strangers have come to the park and kidnapped our children."

"How terrible!" said Majii. "But is there no one protecting the park?"

"A long time ago, our forest, its gorillas, elephants, mountain buffaloes, and all the animals and plants who lived here were protected from hunters and smugglers. Our park sanctuary became the Virunga Park. It's now called the Birunga National Park. Wardens and rangers would patrol the park and protect us. We all felt very safe. Then things began to change, and our park was not the same," explained Mukuru.

Amini, the calm big sister, broke in to introduce herself. Next came Muraho, the father, who always said, "Hello!", and then Ota, the dreamy grandfather with their introductions. Other children played in the background—Tano, Kosa, and Mvua. Finally one last family member spoke up, and everyone fell silent.

"I welcome you, Majii, by telling you my story," said Kosa. "One morning when I was two years old, I strayed away from the family and fell into an antelope trap set by poachers." He slowly raised his left arm and showed Majii that he had no hand. It had been severed. "The trap knocked me unconscious. My brave mother, Uhodari, took great care of me. She kept putting special grass on the open cut."

"That is terrible," sighed Majii, shaking her head. "Just terrible."

"Now when Kosa sees strangers in the forest, he sometimes gets a temper and is very cranky," said Mukuru. "But wouldn't anyone? So many of my own relatives have been either killed or trapped just like Kosa."

"Poachers have often tried to capture our children," said Uhodari in a stern, angry voice.

"Why?" asked Majii.

"Probably to make trophies or to make them into pets," said Mukuru. "Or so we were told!"

"That's so stupid," said Majii. "Have you seen poachers lately?"

"Fewer since a lady living in this forest helped protect our park and all our animal friends," replied Mukuru. "Now we feel much safer, but we are always vigilant."

"Could I see this lady?" asked Majii.

"No, my friend," sighed Mukuru sadly. "She mysteriously died long ago. But others have taken on her work. Until recently our forest was well protected."

Two young gorillas were playing with one another. They rolled happily on the slopes under the watchful eyes of Amini. Some mothers were laying on their backs, talking about their children. Matata was still suckling in his mother's arms. Bahati was pulling roots from the ground for dinner.

Now and then Mukuru grunted gently to remind the frolicking children not to wander too far.

Tano was grooming Kosa. Two young gorillas enjoyed a crunchy watery grass snack. Mvua was hanging from a bamboo stalk, then letting herself drop down. She enjoyed it so much that she did it over and over.

"Aren't you going to hurt yourself?" asked Majii.

"Not at all! I am a pro," said Mvua.

As the sun rose, it became much warmer. The clearing was very quiet except for a gentle breeze whispering through the crowded leaves of the forest trees. Majii looked around as everyone napped. This was a peaceful place.

A little before sunset, Mukuru grunted. It was a signal to make night nests. By the time night fell, the family was sound asleep.

11

In the morning the family got up slowly. They had a mixture of leaves and grass for breakfast. Everybody happily ate their food and enjoyed the bright morning sun. Then Mukuru, Kosa, and Majii went for a long walk to meet Tembo, the mountain elephant.

"Good morning and welcome to our home," Tembo said to Majii. "Before I say anything, let me sprinkle some dust on you with my trunk. It's my way of saying hello!"

Majii thought, "Everyone has their own way of saying hello."

"But where is the rest of your family?" Majii asked.

"To keep my family safe, I sent them to visit their cousins in Zaire. Life is hard here. So many of our trees have been cut down that the weather has changed, and there is not enough rain to make the rivers from which we drink. When I was a baby elephant, my parents thought that this forest had no end. But now there are only small patches of trees, and my family is much smaller. To live, we must travel many miles to find food and water."

"I feel sorry for your family," said Majii. "Can I do anything to help you?"

"We need to teach the world about the beauty of trees and the importance of forests to big and little elephants and big and little animals of all kinds. We need the clouds to bring us more rain so that we can always find food and water near home," said Tembo.

"I am a raindrop! Maybe I can help! I will talk to my friends and family when I get home!" said Majii.

"Do you like our home, Majii?" asked Mukuru.

"Yes, it's so beautiful and different from my home," answered Majii.

"This is where I bring my family to eat bamboo shoots —my favorite meal. When we come here, it is difficult for tourists to find us," said Mukuru with a smile.

"Are tourists visiting you?" asked Majii.

"Once a day, a park ranger brings over a group of tourists. They pay money to see us, which helps keep our home safe," answered Mukuru.

"Are they well behaved?" ventured Majii.

"They better be!" said Kosa. "Otherwise we will teach them a lesson." They all laughed.

Majii, Mukuru, Kosa, and Tembo walked out of the forest. They walked by a few huts, but they were all empty. No children were playing, and no one was cooking.

"But where are the people?" asked Majii.

From behind a hut a little boy appeared. He wore a red shirt and torn khaki pants that were far too short for his growing body. He looked weak and lost. He must be freezing, thought Majii. "What are you doing here, Little One?" asked Mukuru in his deep voice.

The little boy did not answer.

"Who are you?" Majii asked in a soft voice.

"Mutoto," the boy whispered. "I am lost. I walked for the past two days and nights, and I have had no food."

"Three days ago, in the middle of the night, a sudden knock came at my house. All of my family got up, and my father opened the door. There stood a group of men with guns and machetes. They seemed very angry. Their hands were balled into fists, and their eyes were flashing anger. They ordered my family out of our home.

"We know you have been hiding people. Where are they?" the leader said to my father.

"They ran away two days ago," my father answered. The leader pointed a finger at my parents, then two men violently grabbed them.

"Do not kill my son," pleaded my mother. "Let him go. He is innocent." Dad was lost and silent. The men dragged them to a nearby field. I watched them from a distance from the top of a tree I had climbed. The men argued with my parents. Then I heard some snapping sounds and saw my parents fall. The men walked back to our home. I heard the leader order his men to find me. They looked for me and walked several times by the tree where I was hiding, but I kept quiet. They finally walked away. I decided to spend the day in the tree. I was afraid the men would come back. The following night I ran away as fast as I could."

Mutoto was upset after telling his story.

"The land around our park is at war," said Mukuru to Majii.

"From Mutoto's story, it sounds like the people of the country around this park have gone crazy," said Majii.

"You are right," responded Mukuru. "Yet, I have been watching them since I was a kid. They always seemed so peaceful."

"This war seems to be destroying its people and the environment," said Majii. "How do you feel about it, Mukuru?"

Mukuru was silent, thinking.

Majii, Mukuru, Kosa, Tembo, and Mutoto walked to the highest hill. As the sun set in the distance over the lakes and volcanoes, down below on a winding road, they could see a long line of people, adults and children, walking.

"Where are they going?" asked Majii.

"They are running away, trying to escape this bloody war," answered Mutoto. "Some of them have been walking for a week."

Then Majii, Mukuru, Kosa, Tembo, and Mutoto found a quiet wooded area. They decided to stop and spend the night.

Mukuru got up early to make breakfast for Mutoto. It was his first meal in three days. He was getting stronger, and he smiled for the first time.

"Do you want to walk back to our home with us?" asked Majii.

"Yes, I would," said Mutoto.

As they entered the park, they ran into a park warden.

"It's good to see you, Fidel," said Mukuru. "Where are the other wardens and guides? I haven't seen them in a few weeks."

"They ran away with their families," answered Fidel. "They were afraid of the war."

"And why not you, Fidel?" asked Majii.

"That's a different story. I have no family. Besides, if I left, there would be no one to watch our forest, the animals, and especially the gorillas."

"You are so brave!" said Majii.

"I will never leave this park and forest! This is my home, too," Fidel said.

"Could I stay with you, Fidel, and help you?" asked Mutoto.

"Yes! I will take care of you, and you will be my first student," said Fidel with a big smile.

Mutoto jumped for joy and gave Fidel a big hug. "Thank you so much," he said.

Fidel was very pleased and suggested that they stop for the night. Everybody was very tired.

It was a long and interesting walk to the top of the volcano Karisimbi. At first they walked through a bamboo forest. Then Majii saw tall trees from which hair-like lichen hung. The ground was becoming muddy and slippery, and it was getting colder. Majii shivered a bit, hiding in Mukuru's soft fur and wrapping it around herself like a winter coat.

On top of the Karisimbi there was only moss and volcanic rocks, and it was very cold. They could see for miles —the majestic lake Kivu and many rolling green hills. From the top of Karisimbi, it looked like a perfect place.

Majii turned to Mukuru, "Your life is so hard? What could be done to make it easier and to protect your home?"

Mukuru answered, "Majii, you are the only hope left. Will you talk to the children of the world? Children could take the lead in protecting our park. We need no wars. This forest needs protection. We want the people of Rwanda to live together in peace."

"You are so smart, Mukuru. I must start now," smiled Majii with pride. "I will tell the children of this world about my visit and how we can help you. I will go back to my cloud. I will tell my friends of Cumulus Alto about my adventures in your park, then request that the pilot of our cloud take us around the world. We will make stops in schools around the world, where I can meet with other children to spread the word," continued Majii.

"What a good idea," sighed a contented Mukuru. "But what are you going to tell them?"

"I will describe your wonderful park sanctuary, my newly discovered gorilla friends, and the many neighbors living there. I will tell these children about the many problems facing the gorillas and their park."

"What a great visit. Thank you for everything," said Majii emotionally.

A low cloud drifted by, and Mukuru raised his hand in the air with Majii on his palm. Soon they were both in the middle of the cloud.

Majii jumped on to the edges of the cloud.

"Goodbye, my friends," shouted Majii.

As the cloud slowly drifted away, Mukuru and Kosa said goodbye to Majii by beating on their chests. The pok, pok, pok of their fists on their chests echoed all over the land.

FORGING NEW TOMORROWS

Forging New Tomorrows (FNT) International is a non-profit, non-governmental organization dedicated to promoting education, health and environmental protection in developing countries and is formally recognized by, amongst others, the United States Agency for International Development (USAID). Founded in early 1994, this Atlanta based organization was initially created in order to implement a *Post War Rehabilitation & Development Program* for the Ministry of Health of Rwanda and the Rwanda Office of Tourism and National Parks (ORTPN). FNT is an international NGO and operates with delegations in North America, Europe and Africa, including Benin, Burundi, Guinea, Madagascar, Rwanda, and Senegal. Together with its delegates, and in strategic alliance with academic and international institutions and experts in research, education, public health and development, *FNT International* has undertaken a variety of projects in the fields of health research and promotion, conservation and environmental protection, humanitarian relief, and education and technology transfer.

Currently, *FNT International* is preparing for publication of a book entitled *Selected Health Systems of Africa*, endorsed by the Emory University Institute of African Studies, to provide an interdisciplinary approach to understanding existing health systems in Africa. *FNT International* is coordinating an Athletic Training Program to provide educational scholarships and professional training in the USA for athletes from Burundi and Rwanda, under the guidance of Dieudonné Kwizera, a former world class middle distance runner and coach of the first, and only, olympic gold medal winner from Burundi. *FNT International* is also in the process of developing a range of education and media development projects in remembrance of the 1994 genocide in Rwanda and in support of peace and reconciliation initiatives in Rwanda, Burundi and several other African countries.

The publication of *Majii and the Mountain Gorillas of Rwanda* is a source of great pride to us at FNT. This project represents the outcome of a unique educational and creative collaboration between Marc Daniel Gutekunst and Stan Mullins (two founding members of FNT International), the *Dian Fossey Gorilla Fund International,* deeply committed educators, passionate parents and, most importantly, several hundred inspired and inspiring elementary and high school students. We hope that the involvement of the children in the making of the book, educating them about the gorillas, their natural habitat and their interaction with people, as well as providing them with creative means of making a difference, both individually and collectively, shall inspire others to use the professional and personal concerns of parents and local institutions to complement the public school curriculum in its endeavor to introduce children to a diverse, complex, and exciting world beyond the classroom.

Proceeds from the sale of the book will be donated to the *Dian Fossey Gorilla Fund International* to provide scholarships to Rwandan students committed to the conservation of wildlife in Rwanda.

Cheryl Williams
Epidemiologist, Centers for Disease Control and Prevention in Atlanta, and
Member of the Board of Directors
Forging New Tomorrows, Inc.

Forging New Tomorrows, Inc.
A Non-Profit Organization
1534 North Decatur Road, Suite 204
Atlanta, GA 30307
USA
1 (404) 636-5888
http://www.fnt-usa.org

The **Dian Fossey**
Gorilla Fund International

OVERVIEW

The Dian Fossey Gorilla Fund International (DFDF) was founded by the late Dr. Dian Fossey to support her conservation and research activities on behalf of the mountain gorilla. Based at the Karisoke Research Center, Rwanda, and made famous by the movie "Gorillas in the Mist," Dian Fossey's life and tragic death captured the attention of millions of people around the world.

KARISOKE RESEARCH CENTER

Directed by a series of internationally renowned field scientists and staffed by research assistants and trackers, the Karisoke Research Center has been a force in gorilla conservation since 1967. The trackers are skilled in gorilla observation and habituation, assisting scientists with data collection and monitoring permanent biodiversity inventory plots. Several of them are long term (20+ years) employees of DFGF International and have finely honed skills and experience. They are experts at tracking poachers and in finding and removing their snares, as well as using Geographic Positioning System units. Their skills and experience have been used by several other projects in the region to assist in gorilla habituation, ranger training, and census and Geographic Information System (GIS) training.

KARISOKE COMMUNITY

The aftermath of the war and genocide in Rwanda in 1994 created many orphans and left many elderly without immediate family members. Our Karisoke Community includes not only our trackers' immediate families, but also nieces, nephews, cousins, and some who are unable to care for themselves - a total of 260 men, women and children. We have begun a series of small self-sustaining projects, which will make the people less dependent on the land for survival. We also have an education fund for the children of Karisoke trackers.

FIELD CONSERVATION

Like the mountain gorilla, many of the world's most endangered species live in parts of the world beset by political strife and unrest. Fieldwork is, therefore, difficult without a trained work force of local people and the ability of field researchers to transmit data quickly and accurately to a scientific base and to local National Park authorities.

During 1998, we began the process of forming the Institute for Conservation, Research and Technology, a collaboration of the Georgia Institute of Technology, Zoo Atlanta, Clark Atlanta University and the Dian Fossey Gorilla Fund International in the USA, and the National University of Rwanda and National Parks Authorities in Africa.

The purpose of the initial project is to apply the joint technological, scientific, education and conservation strengths of the collaborators to a field project. This will involve the development and deployment of appropriate technologies in the field and the formalization of in-country partnerships. These are essential to defining the conservation priorities of the park authorities and to building the long-term science, conservation and technology infrastructure of the Central East Africa region. The first phase comprises a field project in Rwanda, in the Volcanoes National Park. We will then expand the proven elements of the present project to a regional level and the creation of a center for GIS and remote sensing in Rwanda.

PUBLIC INFORMATION, EDUCATION, AND ADVOCACY

The Fund's education, outreach, marketing and fundraising activities depend on and emanate from its store of scientific ideas, programs, and archived materials. The program's valuable archived field photo and video materials are used by numerous media organizations, providing revenue for the Fund in addition to serving as a powerful education and marketing tool. A curriculum for classroom teachers is undergoing its first revision, with plans for updating and interactive media components to be added. A first review by teachers is complete. In Rwanda, DFGF International has a long history of support for local schools and an ongoing collaboration with the National University of Rwanda, with funding for visiting professors, student stipends and equipment.

The **Dian Fossey**
Gorilla Fund International

800 Cherokee Avenue, SE
Atlanta, Georgia 30315-9984
USA
1 (800) 851-0203

http://www.gorillafund.org